# The Mole Sisters
## and the Rainy Day

written and illustrated by Roslyn Schwartz

Annick Press Ltd.
Toronto • New York • Vancouver

© 1999 Roslyn Schwartz (text and illustrations)
Cover design by Sheryl Shapiro
Third printing, March 2002
Annick Press Ltd.
All rights reserved. No part of this work covered by the copyrights hereon may be reproduced or used in any form or by any means – graphic, electronic, or mechanical – without the prior written permission of the publisher.

We acknowledge the support of the Canada Council for the Arts, the Ontario Arts Council, and the Government of Canada through the Book Publishing Industry Development Program (BPIDP) for our publishing activities.

**Cataloging in Publication Data**

Schwartz, Roslyn
  The mole sisters and the rainy day

(The mole sisters series)
ISBN 1-55037-611-X (bound)   ISBN 1-55037-610-1 (pbk.)

I. Title. II. Series: Schwartz, Roslyn. Mole sisters series.

PS8587.C5785M643 1999          jC813'.54          C99-930676-6
PZ7.S38Mol 1999

The art in this book was rendered in colored pencils.
The text was typeset in Apollo.

Distributed in Canada by:              Published in the U.S.A. by Annick Press (U.S.) Ltd.
Firefly Books Ltd.                     Distributed in the U.S.A. by:
3680 Victoria Park Avenue              Firefly Books (U.S.) Inc.
Willowdale, ON                         P.O. Box 1338, Ellicott Station
M2H 3K1                                Buffalo, NY 14205

Printed and bound in Canada by Kromar Printing Ltd., Winnipeg, Manitoba.

**visit us at: www.annickpress.com**

To Mattia and Rowan.

"What a lovely day,"
said the mole sisters.

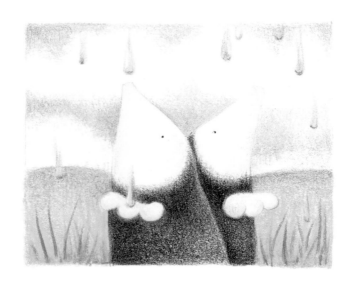

Until it started to rain.

"Never mind," they said.

"It won't last."

But it did.

WHOOSH

"Yikes!"

Down their hole they went.

KERPLUNK

"Hey?"

"Oh Oh."

"Never mind," they said.
"It won't last."

But it did.

"Now what?"

"Of course."

"Well done."

"Tum, Tee, Tum, Tee Ta ..."

"Perfect."

And they splished

and splashed

until the sun came out

and the rain stopped.

"See?"

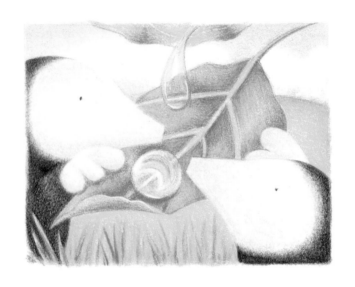

"We were right."

"It didn't last long after all."

"What a lovely day," said
the mole sisters.

And it was!

Also about the Mole Sisters: